Katie Woo

Katie Woo, Where Are You?

by Fran Manushkin
illustrated by Tammie Lyon

PICTURE WINDOW BOOKS
a capstone imprint

Katie Woo is published by Picture Window Books
151 Good Counsel Drive, P.O. Box 669
Mankato, Minnesota 56002
www.capstonepub.com

Library of Congress Cataloging-in-Publication Data
Manushkin, Fran.
Katie Woo, where are you? / by Fran Manushkin; illustrated by Tammie Lyon.
p. cm. — (Katie Woo)
Summary: While shopping with her parents in a mall, Katie helps a lost boy, not realizing that she may be lost, too.
ISBN 978-1-4048-6517-4 (library binding)
ISBN 978-1-4048-6853-3 (pbk.)
[1. Lost children—Fiction. 2. Shopping—Fiction. 3. Chinese Americans—Fiction.] I. Lyon, Tammie, ill. II. Title.
PZ7.M3195Kbm 2011
[E]—dc22 2011005490

Art Director: Kay Fraser
Graphic Designer: Emily Harris

Printed in the United States of America in Melrose Park, Illinois.
032011
006112LKF11

Table of Contents

Chapter 1
A Trip to the Mall 5

Chapter 2
Where's Katie? 12

Chapter 3
A Happy Ending 22

Chapter 1

A Trip to the Mall

Katie Woo was watching a TV show about a lost baby whale. Suddenly, the picture went out!

Her dad tried to fix it. "It's too old," he said. "We need a new TV."

"I need a party dress," said Katie's mom. "Let's go to the mall."

"I guess I'll never know if the whale mom found her baby," Katie sighed.

The mall was only ten minutes away.

Katie's mom said, "While I try on dresses, you and your dad can check out the TVs."

Katie walked in front of her dad. Suddenly he stopped and said, “Look at these neat lawn mowers!”

But Katie didn’t hear him. Someone was talking on the loud speaker.

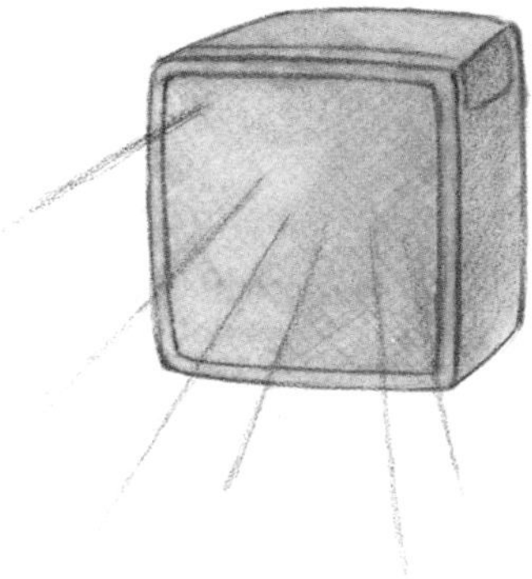

"We are looking for a lost boy," said the speaker. "He has blond hair and is wearing a red T-shirt. His name is Teddy. If you find him, bring him to the Lost and Found."

"Poor Teddy," said Katie. "It's awful to be lost."

Katie did not notice that her dad was gone. She was looking at the TVs. They all showed the end of Katie's program about the whale.

"Hurray!" Katie said. "His mom found him! I hope someone finds Teddy."

Chapter 2

Where's Katie?

"I'd like to be a TV star,"

Katie decided.

She put

on sunglasses,

a pretty scarf,

and a big, floppy hat.

Katie walked past her dad. He did not know it was her under the fancy glasses, scarf, and hat.

Katie did not see her dad, either.

Katie walked past her mom, trying on a dress. They did not notice each other.

"I look awesome!" said Katie, looking into a mirror.

"I look awful," said her mother, looking into a mirror, too.

Katie passed a blond boy in a red T-shirt. He was crying.

She stopped and asked, "Is your name Teddy?"

"Yes," he sniffled.

"Yay!" Katie said. "I found the lost boy."

At that same moment, Katie's mom asked her dad, "Where's Katie?"

"Oh, no!" said her dad. "I thought she was with you."

Katie found the Lost and Found. "Here's Teddy," she said proudly. "I found him."

"Good for you," said the lady. "But now somebody else is lost."

She said on the loud speaker, "We are looking for a lost girl. She has dark hair and her name is Katie Woo. If you find her, bring her to the Lost and Found."

Katie laughed. "I'm not lost!" she said. "I'm right here!"

Chapter 3

A Happy Ending

Katie's parents were so happy to see her!

"Guess what?" Katie told them. "The baby whale's mom found her too! And I found Teddy."

"I love happy endings," said her mom.

"But we still have to get the TV and the dress," said Katie's dad.

"I'll lead the way," Katie offered. "I know where everything is."

And this time, nobody got lost.

SUPER
MALL

About the Author

Fran Manushkin is the author of many popular picture books, including *How Mama Brought the Spring; Baby, Come Out!; Latkes and Applesauce: A Hanukkah Story;* and *The Tushy Book*. There is a real Katie Woo — she's Fran's great-niece — but she never gets in half the trouble of the Katie Woo in the books. Fran writes on her beloved Mac computer in New York City, without the help of her two naughty cats, Miss Chippie and Goldy.

About the Illustrator

Tammie Lyon began her love for drawing at a young age while sitting at the kitchen table with her dad. She continued her love of art and eventually attended the Columbus College of Art and Design, where she earned a bachelors degree in fine art. After a brief career as a professional ballet dancer, she decided to devote herself full time to illustration. Today she lives with her husband, Lee, in Cincinnati, Ohio. Her dogs, Gus and Dudley, keep her company as she works in her studio.

Glossary

awesome (AW-suhm)—causing a feeling of wonder or respect

awful (AW-fuhl)—terrible or horrible

hurray (huh-RAY)—a word used when people cheer

offered (OF-urd)—asked someone if he or she would like something

sighed (SYED)—breathed out deeply, often to express sadness or relief

suddenly (SUHD-uhn-lee)—quickly

Discussion Questions

1. Did Katie want to go to the mall? Explain your answer.

2. How did Katie get lost? Have you ever gotten lost or separated from your parents?

3. Katie didn't even notice that she was lost. Why not?

Writing Prompts

1. Katie and her parents read a map so they knew where to go in the store. Draw a map of your classroom, yard, or bedroom. Be sure to write labels for important things or areas.

2. Katie wore a sort of disguise in this story. Draw a picture of yourself in a disguise, then write a story to explain why you are dressed up.

3. The woman at the Lost and Found had to describe the lost boy. She talked about his shirt and hair color. Write a description of yourself that could be used if you were lost.

Having Fun with Katie Woo!

Guess Who!

When a boy or girl gets lost at the mall, a description of him or her is often used so others can keep an eye out for the person who is missing. Besides being fun, this game will give you practice at using words that describe.

What you need:

- a partner
- 10 to 20 photos of people or characters who are familiar to both you and your partner. You could use people from your school, famous people, or cartoon and book characters.